BREVARD COUNTY LIBRARIES

3 2490 0008 8967 0

COCOA BEACH PUBLIC LIBRARY

P9-CCZ-013

· This BOOK belongs to ·

_____

_____

COCOA BEACH PUBLIC LIBRARY
550 NO. BREVARD AVENUE
COCOA BEACH, FL 32931

RETURN POSTAGE GUARANTEED IF
RETURNED TO ANY LIBRARY IN THE U.S.

PROPERTY OF
BREVARD COUNTY LIBRARY SYSTEM
DEMCO

For Benjamin — P.K.

**For Woongsun and Hyunmin,
and special thanks to Meehyun Paik** — T.Y.

Copyright © 2014 by Polly Kanevsky
Jacket art and interior illustrations © 2014 by Taeeun Yoo

All rights reserved. Published in the United States by Schwartz & Wade Books,
an imprint of Random House Children's Books, a division of Random House LLC, a Penguin Random House Company, New York.
Schwartz & Wade Books and the colophon are trademarks of Random House LLC.

Visit us on the Web! randomhouse.com/kids
Educators and librarians, for a variety of teaching tools, visit us at RHTeachersLibrarians.com

Library of Congress Cataloging-in-Publication Data
Kanevsky, Polly.
Here is the baby / Polly Kanevsky ; illustrated by Taeeun Yoo.—1st ed.
p. cm.
Summary: Follows a day in the life of a baby as he wakes up to the morning sun,
has breakfast, goes with his father to the library and the grocery store, plays, has dinner, and finally goes to bed.
ISBN 978-0-375-86731-6 (trade) — ISBN 978-0-375-96731-3 (glb)
ISBN 978-0-375-98785-4 (ebook)
[1. Babies—Fiction. 2. Family life—Fiction.] I. Yoo, Taeeun, ill. II. Title.
PZ7.K12763He 2013
[E]—dc23
2011011021

The text of this book is set in Memphis LT Std.
Book design by Polly Kanevsky
The illustrations were rendered using linoleum block prints, pencil drawings, and Adobe Photoshop.

MANUFACTURED IN CHINA
10 8 6 4 2 1 3 5 7 9
First Edition

Random House Children's Books supports the First Amendment and celebrates the right to read.

Here is the Baby

written by **Polly Kanevsky**   illustrated by **Taeeun Yoo**

COCOA BEACH PUBLIC LIBRARY

550 NO. BREVARD AVENUE

COCOA BEACH, FL 32931

schwartz **&** wade books • new york

Here is the baby.
And a bright
morning sun.

Shhh, says the mama,
and brings Baby close.

Here is the baby,
hungry and wet.
Mama changes his diaper.
She gives him some milk.

Here is the daddy,
cutting slices of melon.

He butters the toast and spoons cherry jam.

Here is the sister, ready for school.
She whispers a secret and sings Baby's song.

Now here is the baby.
He's trying to walk.

Here is the daddy.
He holds Baby's hands.

Here is the baby. He's trying to talk.
Here is the neighbor. She says Baby's name.

Here are the steps
to the library door.

Here is the lady.
She reads to the children.

Here's the old lady
who lives in a shoe.

And here is the cow
jumping over the moon.

Here is the baby.
He looks for that moon.

And here is the baby.
He wants to see more.

But here is a baby
who's starting to fuss.
And here is a baby who's
rubbing his eyes.

So here is the daddy.
He scoops Baby up.

Now Baby
wants biscuits.
And Baby
wants pear.

Now here is
that baby,
wrapped
tight in his
blanket.

Here is the baby, in the afternoon sun.

And here is the grocer.
And here is the postman.
A truck rumbles by.

Shhh, Baby, shhh.

Now here are some children,
laughing and playing.

Their sounds fill
the air.

Baby opens his eyes.

Here is the baby
hunting for treasures.

Here is the daddy
helping him climb.

Now the sun's disappearing.
The air's getting cooler.

But where's Baby's mitten?
And where is his mama?

Here is the baby.
He wants to
go home.

Here is
the daddy.
He keeps
Baby warm.

Here is the sister.

And there's that green mitten.

Here is the mama.

The baby is home.

Now here is the baby.
He's ready for dinner.

Here is the soup,
in a heavy red pot.

Here is the baby.
He picks up a green bean.

And here's Baby's carrot. He doesn't want help.

Here are Sister and Baby,
with a blue china tea set.
But here is the mama.
She scoots them along.

Here are the bubbles.
The window's all steamy.

Here's Mama with towels.
She wraps Baby tight.

Here are kisses from Sister.
Here are kisses from Daddy.

Now here is that baby.
He's ready for sleep.

And here is the mama.
She scoops Baby up.

She brings Baby close
and gives him some milk.

She wraps Baby tight
to keep Baby warm.

She reads him a book,

then sings Baby's song.

Mama holds Baby's hand.

Mama
whispers
his name.

Here is the baby.

Shhh, Baby, shhh.